For Claudia Kemp   H.O.
For Jenny, Colin and baby Kirsten   M.R.

Text copyright © Hiawyn Oram 1992
Illustrations copyright © Mary Rees 1992

First published in Great Britain in 1992 by
Frances Lincoln Limited, 4 Torriano Mews
Torriano Avenue, London NW5 2RZ

British Library Cataloguing in Publication Data available on request

ISBN 0-7112-0682-1 paperback

Printed in Hong Kong

7 9 8

MINE!

Hiawyn Oram

Illustrated by
Mary Rees

FRANCES LINCOLN

Isabel went to play with Claudia.
She climbed onto Claudia's rocking horse.

"Mine!" shrieked Claudia and pushed her off.

Isabel picked up Claudia's Carrot Top doll.

"Mine!" screamed Claudia and snatched
it away.

Isabel saw Claudia's wooden animals
piled up in an old shoebox. She took them
out and set them up on the carpet.

"No, no, no!" cried Claudia. "My moo cows. My baa lambs!"

Claudia's mother put on their hats and
coats and gloves and scarves.
"What we need is some fresh air," she said.

Isabel and Claudia and Claudia's mother walked to the park. Claudia's mother pushed Claudia's new tricycle.

When they got to the park Isabel climbed
onto the tricycle.

"No no no!" yelled Claudia. "My bike,
my bike. Me! Me! Me!"
She pulled Isabel off the tricycle.

"Now Claudia, let Izzie have a turn,"
said Claudia's mother.
"No Izzie, no Izzie," screamed Claudia.

"Mine! Mine! Mine!" And she pushed
the tricycle out of Isabel's reach.
It ran down the hill.
   It ran faster and faster.
       It rolled over and over.

They watched the bell fly off
and land in a bird's nest.

They watched the handlebars fly off
and land in a tree.

They watched the saddle fly off and land
in the bandstand and the saddlebag land
in a baby's pram.

They watched the wheels come off
and roll, one by one, into the road,
into the pond,

and into the park-keeper's hut.

They watched nuts and bolts and screws
and chains spray into the air and across
the grass and disappear forever into piles
of leaves.

They ran down the hill

and stood staring at the battered broken
new tricycle frame . . .

"Yours," said Isabel
and went to feed the ducks.

MORE PICTURE BOOKS IN PAPERBACK
FROM FRANCES LINCOLN

LITTLE BROTHER AND THE COUGH
Hiawyn Oram
Illustrated by Mary Rees

When a new baby arrives in the family, it's not always easy.
In this case it leads to a Cough, a very bad Cough, a very very VERY Bad Cough!
Poor big sister. No one seems to notice how she feels...
until at last the Cough becomes desperate, and people listen to it and soothe it.
And suddenly, a little girl finds that she can talk to her baby brother, after all.

Suitable for National Curriculum English — Reading, Key Stages 1 and 2
Scottish Guidelines English Language — Reading, Level A

ISBN 0-7112-0845-X £5.99

ELEPHANTS DON'T DO BALLET
Penny McKinlay
Illustrated by Graham Percy

When Esmeralda the elephant wants to be a ballerina,
Mummy's not so sure – after all, elephants don't do ballet.
But Esmeralda joins a ballet class. She gets her trunk in a tangle,
but goes on triumphantly to prove that elephants can do ballet!

Suitable for National Curriculum English — Reading, Key Stage 1
Scottish Guidelines English Language — Reading, Level A

ISBN 0-7112-1130-2 £4.99

AMAZING GRACE!
Mary Hoffman
Illustrated by Caroline Binch

Grace loves to act out stories, so when there's the chance to play
a part in Peter Pan, Grace longs to play Peter. But her classmates
say that Peter was a boy, and besides, he wasn't black...
With the support of her mother and grandmother, however,
Grace soon discovers that if you set your mind to it, you can
do anything that you want to.

Chosen as part of the recommended booklist for the National Curriculum
Key Stage 1, English Task, Reading, Level 2
Scottish Guidelines English Language — Reading, Level B

ISBN 0-7112-0699-6 £5.99

Frances Lincoln titles are available from all good bookshops.
Prices are correct at time of publication, but may be subject to change.